LAURA OWEN & KORKY PAUL

Winnie AND Wilbur

Giddy-up
WINNIE

OXFORD
UNIVERSITY PRESS

CONTENTS

WINNIE'S
Tea Party

53

Giddy-up,
WINNIE

75

WINNIE'S
Wheels

Yawn! went Winnie standing in her sloth slippers, watching raindrops slide down the window like baby snails.

'It's raining, it's pouring,

my cat is snoring.

This is so blooming

boring, boring, boring!'

Winnie put fingers on two different raindrops on the other side of the window. She followed the drops downwards to see which drop would win.

7

'Drippy-drop won!' she said. Wilbur opened one eye, then closed it again, and yawned widely, showing his fangs.

Winnie took a pongberry from the fruit bowl and she threw it at Wilbur.

'Mrrow!'

'Let's *do* something!' said Winnie. 'I know, I'll ring Jerry next door and see if he'd like to come and play Crocodile Snap or Crabbage.'

But, 'I'm just packin' to go on holiday, missus,' said Jerry down the telling moan. 'Toodle pip.'

'Holiday?!' said Winnie. 'A holiday, Wilbur! That's exactly what we need. We'll get away for a nice holiday!'

Suddenly Winnie had energy again. 'Abracadabra!'

A pile of holiday brochures landed on
the table. Winnie pounced on them.
'Come on, Wilbur! Help me choose!'

Winnie found holidays by the sea.
'Lovely!' said Winnie.

'Mrrow!' said Wilbur.

'You've had enough of wetness from all
this rain, have you?' said Winnie. 'This
one looks dry!' she said, waving a picture
of an African plain with lions prowling.

'Meeeow!' squeaked Wilbur.

'Don't you like cats that big?' said
Winnie. 'Where do you want to go, then?'

Wilbur pointed at a holiday for old
people which showed a fat cat lying
snoozing in front of a fire.

'That'd be about as exciting as watching
the Snail Olympics!' said Winnie.

II

'Oh, dear! Perhaps I should just leave
you with my sister Wanda and her cat
Wayne while I go on holiday on my own?'

'MRRRROW!' said Wilbur, his eyes
opening wide and his claws clinging
tightly to the tatty rat-leather chair he was
sitting on.

'Oh, all right! Don't get your whiskers
in a whizz!' said Winnie. 'I'd rather have a

holiday with you. But where can we go
where we'll both be happy?' Then—
zing!—'I've got it!' she said. 'Let's go on
a mystery tour!'

'Meeow?' said Wilbur.

'You know,' said Winnie. 'A journey
where we just set off and keep going until
we find somewhere we like. Then we stop
and enjoy it.'

Wilbur did a claws-up sign, so that was
decided.

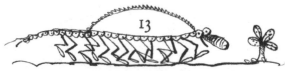

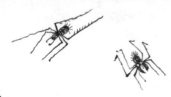

Winnie got packing.

'Elephant snorkel and seal flippers in case we go in the sea. A bunny-bonnet hat and skunk boots in case we find snow. Squashed-fly biscuits and best mouldy-oldy cheese and radish-reptile relish in case we don't like the food when we get there. Midge attraction cream, crocodile bite lotion, a waiter-charming potion, pig crackling oinkment for sunburn. A tent and pegs and matches and pans and . . . oh,' said Winnie. 'This bag isn't going to be anywhere near big enough.'

Winnie filled a suitcase too, and a trunk. Then Wilbur came staggering along with his backpack full of fish-fin bits and his comfy-wumfy blanket and his sun

glasses and his goggles and his maps and
his tin opener and his whisker cream.

'Pile it all in, Wilbur!' said Winnie.
'We'll manage somehow!'

They staggered outside with their
luggage, and were instantly soaked.

'Tut! That's another thing!' said
Winnie, running back inside.
'I forgot my umbrella and my
smelly-wellies!'

They climbed onto Winnie's broomstick.
'Off we go, Broom!' shouted Winnie.
'Take us wherever you like! Oooo, this is
exciting! I wonder where we'll end up!'

Heave! went Broom. **Strain-tug-heave!** Nothing moved.

The poor broomstick just couldn't lift such a weight of luggage. 'Well, we can't leave our luggage behind,' said Winnie. 'There's only one thing for it!' Winnie waved her wand, *swish-swish!*

'Abracadabra!'

And suddenly there was a car parked in
front of her house.

'Oooo! Isn't it shiny! Isn't it handsome?
And big! With a boot for the luggage!
And a roof to keep the rain out! Why
didn't I think of getting a car before?'

'Meeow!' agreed Wilbur.

Winnie began to throw luggage into the

boot, and tie it onto the roof, and hang it from the door handles. 'Hecking hippopotamus! We still need more room! I know what!' **Swish!** went Winnie's wand again.

'Abracadabra!'

And instantly there was a fine witch caravan behind the car.

'Perfect!' said Winnie, throwing her  broomstick into the caravan. 'Now, we're ready for anything! Get into the car, Wilbur! I'll get the heating going, and the windscreen vipers, then off we brolly well go!'

But Winnie didn't know her windscreen viper knob from her headlight dipper. She didn't know her gear stick from her brake pedal from her toad horn.

Suddenly there were lights flashing and horns honking and engines revving. Wilbur's fur was standing on end!

'Driving a car really can't be that difficult!' said Winnie, prodding a big button on the dashboard. 'Lots of idiots manage it!' **Lurch! Leap! St-st-st-stagger-stop!**

'It's like a blasted kangaroo!' said Winnie. 'Stupid thing!'

'MMMMMMMMmew!' whimpered Wilbur.

'What?' said Winnie. 'You want me to give up? Just one more try, eh?'

Prod, kick, turn, yank. Vrrroooom! The car lurched backwards this time, bumping the caravan—

thump-bump-lump-lump-lump!

'Ooooooer!' said Winnie. 'We're going backwards and the road only goes

forwards! Errr! Hold tight, Wilbur! We're going dowwnnn the hiillll.' **Crump!**

'Oh,' said Winnie.

The car and caravan had come to a halt beside the duck pond at the bottom of Winnie's garden. Their wheels were sinking into the mud, completely stuck.

'Oh,' said Winnie again.

Wilbur stepped out of the car. He was
trembling. His eyes were huge. Winnie took
one look at him. 'Er . . .Wilbur, shall we
just stay and have our holiday here?'

'Meeow!' said Wilbur, nodding fiercely.

The rain had stopped and the sun was
just coming out. Winnie and Wilbur set
up their tent and sorted their belongings.

'We can snorkel in the pond,' said

Winnie. 'We can climb that tree! We can do anything we blooming well want to do!'

They toasted marsh-smellows over the stove. 'We've got all our favourite things!' said Winnie. 'And when it's time to go home, we don't even have to drive there!'

'Meeow!' said Wilbur, wiping a paw across his forehead.

'It's almost perfect!' said Winnie.

'All that's missing is a bit of company.'

Then suddenly there was a **THUD THUD THUDDING** sound and, 'Hullo, missus!' said a voice.

'Jerry!' said Winnie. 'I thought you were going on holiday!'

'I've gone!' said Jerry. 'I *is* on holiday. Look at what I'm wearin'!'

'Then come and join us for a drinky-goo, Jerry,' said Winnie. 'And then we'll have a mudcastle making competition—you and Scruff against me and Wilbur.'

So they did. Who do you think was the winner?

Blooming
WINNIE

Squeaky-squeaky-squeak-eek!

'Who's maddening a mouse?' said Winnie, looking up from her breakfast toast and mildew marmalade spread. 'Oh, it's my blooming mobile moan! Have you been playing with the ringtones again, Wilbur?' Winnie snatched the phone from her pocket and put it to her ear. 'Hello?'

A ladylike voice on the phone said, 'This is Mrs Parmar from the school. I have a favour to ask.'

'Oh, yes?' said Winnie.

'Yes,' said Mrs Parmar. 'Could the schoolchildren come and look at plants and creatures in your garden, Winnie? They're doing a project.'

'Oooo, that'd be lovely!' said Winnie. 'Little ordinaries in my garden!'

'There is one rule!' said Mrs Parmar sternly.

'What's that then?' said Winnie.

'You must absolutely do absolutely no magic at all while the children are absolutely with you.'

'Easy-peasy pink-worm-squeezy!' said Winnie.

'I'm trusting you, Winnie!' said Mrs Parmar. 'I'll bring the children at two o'clock.'

31

'Yippee!' said Winnie, trying to dance with Wilbur. Then she looked out of the window. 'Oh,' she said. 'Ooo, dear. I'd forgotten what a tangle-mangle the garden is.' Winnie began to pull her wand from her sleeve. 'Mrs P didn't say, "No magic *before* the little ordinaries arrive". Let's do some wand-gardening, Wilbur!'

Wilbur followed her outside.

'Children will want frilly-flowery, sweet-smelly, bright-colouredy kinds of things,' said Winnie, waving her wand.

'Abracadabra!'

33

And instantly Winnie was wearing
the most frilly-flowery, sweet-smelly,
bright-colouredy shoes you've ever seen.

'Blooming bats' bottoms!' said Winnie.
'What's gone wrong?'

Wilbur sniggered behind a paw, and pointed at Winnie's wand. The wand was bent.

'It's pointing to the wrong blooming thing!' said Winnie. 'Let's try again! *Abracadabra!*'

And instantly the big black crows
sitting in the trees became frilly-flowery,
sweet-smelly, bright-colouredy birds.

'That's not right!' said Winnie, trying
to straighten her wand. But it just wilted
again. 'What in the witchy world is wrong
with my wand?'

Winnie tried stroking the wand. 'Don't oo feel very well, wandy?' The wand stayed wilted. Winnie bandaged the wand. She dipped the wand in medicine. But it stayed wilted. 'I've run out of ideas,' said Winnie. 'Let's look in Great Aunt Winifred's *Book of All Things Magic* and see if she knows how to cure it.'

Winnie opened the dusty book and looked at the spells inside.

'Oh, heck and botheration!' she said. 'I can't read this curly piggy tails kind of writing! Oh, I wish my great auntie who lived so long ago and was so wise could help me. I was named after her, you know, Wilbur, but I've never been as clever as her.'

'Buck yourself up, gal!' said a dusty old voice. *Cough, cough!*

'Oooer!' said Winnie.

'Hisss!' went Wilbur, all prickles and
big eyes.

Because there, looming like grey smog
floating over the table, was Winnie's Great
Aunt Winifred.

'What's your problem, gal?' she boomed.

'Ug. Er, gnn,' said Winnie who had forgotten how to talk.

'Spit it out!' said the spectre.

'It's my wand,' said Winnie. 'It's wilted.'

'Booster's wand food will soon sort it!' said Winifred.

'I've tried that,' said Winnie. 'I've tried everything! Nothing works!'

'Don't despair, gal,' said Great Aunt Winifred. 'Just grow yerself a new wand, don't-ya know.'

'Really?' said Winnie.

'As easy as picking fleas from a fairy cake,' said Winifred. 'Shove yer wand into some soil. Water it. Give it some sunshine. Watch it grow. Simple as that.'

'Cor,' said Winnie. 'I never knew.'

Winnie planted her wilted wand, and gave it water and sunshine, and it began to grow. It grew up and out, growing fat wands, thin wands, knobbly wands, curvy wands, wibbly-wobbly wands.

42

'Just pick one good straight one. That's
the ticket!' said Great Aunt Winifred,
floating just behind Winnie's right ear.

Winnie was just reaching out to pick a
perfect wand, when they heard something.

'Sounds like a hundred screeching owl
chicks, just popped from their eggs!' said
Great Aunt Winifred, covering her ears.

'It's the little ordinaries!' said Winnie.
'Get into the house, Auntie! They mustn't
see you!'

43

'Here are the children, Winnie!' said
Mrs Parmar. 'I'll collect them at three
o'clock. Have a good afternoon, and
remember . . .'

'No magic!' said Winnie. 'I know.'

But the little ordinaries didn't seem to
know about that rule. They weren't
interested in the giant rhubarb and custard
plant crawling with cattypillars. They
weren't interested in stinking nettles or
the tangle-vines or the bulging bugle bugs.
No. The little ordinaries ran straight to
the wand tree and began picking wands,
and waving wands, and . . .

44

'Oh, I don't think . . .!' began Winnie,
but nobody was listening. 'Oh, dimpled
slug bottoms, whatever shall I do, Wilbur?
Wilbur?'

But Wilbur wasn't at Winnie's feet
any more. Instead there was a small
sad-looking black mammoth. 'Wilbur!'
cried Winnie in anguish. 'Oh, please
little ordinaries, don't . . .'

Zip! Zap! Ting! Splosh! Zob!

Magic was flying everywhere. Plants
were being changed. Children were being
changed. Winnie was being changed!

Then Great Aunt Winifred came
wafting to the rescue. She roared into
the garden like cross fog.

46

'Desist! At once!' she told the children in a voice that echoed from the house walls.

The children did desist. They froze, their mouths open.

'Place every wand on the ground!' boomed Winifred. 'Now, line up, two by two. Backs straight! No talking!'

Great Aunt Winifred picked up one good straight wand.

'Abracadabra!'

And instantly Winnie and Wilbur were
back to being themselves. Just in time,
because there was Mrs Parmar hurrying
along to fetch the children.

'Oh, my goodness!' said Mrs Parmar
when she saw the children. 'They *are*
being well-behaved! You didn't do any
magic on them, did you, Winnie?'

'*I've* not done any magic all afternoon,'
said Winnie.

'Good!' said Mrs Parmar. 'Back to
school then, children! My goodness,
how quiet you are! Well done, Winnie!'

'Phew in a shrew stew!' said Winnie as
the children disappeared. 'Shall we have a
bonfire of all those wands?'

So Winnie and Wilbur and Great Aunt
Winifred enjoyed a bonfire that burned
every colour and sparked magical sounds
and smells and spooks and surprises while
they toasted squish-mellows.

At bedtime Winifred began to tell Winnie, 'Brush your hair one hundred strokes, gal! And put on a corset for bed or you'll end up with no figure! Have you polished . . .?'

'Time to go back in your book, Auntie,' said Winnie. 'Nighty-night. Mind the book worms don't bite!' She slammed it shut. And then there was silence.

'Ah!' said Winnie.

'Meeowwah!' agreed Wilbur.

WINNIE'S
Tea Party

Scrunch-flap-munch-crunch!

'The blooming letter box is scoffing the post again. Quick!' shouted Winnie.

Wilbur leapt to rescue a postcard dangling from the letter box's teeth.

'Let me see!' said Winnie. 'Ooo, look! "Pyramids at sunset" from Cousin Cuthbert. I haven't seen Cuthbert since . . . Ooo, Wilbur, let's invite him to tea! And let's invite Uncle Owen and Auntie Alice, too!'

53

Wilbur made a face.

'We'll send the invitations by parrot-post,' said Winnie. *'Abracadabra!'*

Instantly there were three parrots flapping and squawking all around the room, knocking everything over.

'Come and perch on my wand, parrots,' said Winnie. 'Shut your silly beaks and listen. You're to go to Cousin Cuthbert and Uncle Owen and Auntie Alice, and ask them all if they'd like to come for tea today. Flap-off, and bring me back the replies!'

With green, yellow, orange, and red
feathers flying everywhere, the birds flew
away. Winnie was just picking up feathers
and trying them in her hair when there
was a peck-peck sound at the door, and
three parrot voices saying, 'Open the
door, open the door, open the door.'

'I think I'd better open the door,' said Winnie, and she let the parrots in.

'Cuthbert can come,' said the first parrot.

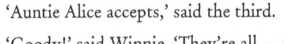

'Owen OK,' said the second.

'Auntie Alice accepts,' said the third.

'Goody!' said Winnie. 'They're all coming! I'd better get cooking!'

Winnie set to work. She thumped and
squashed and pulled and squirted, and
shoved lots of tins into the oven.

'Lots of lovely food,' said Winnie,
licking a mixing spoon. 'Yum!'

Smoke rose from the oven behind her.

'Meow!' said Wilbur.

'Oh, wombat wellies!' said Winnie,
grabbing the yeti fur oven mitt. The
rhubarb and rat-tail buns weren't too
badly burned, but Winnie was all of a
fluster. As she swung round with her oven
mitt—**thwack, crash, shatter!**

'Oh, no! The teapot's in pieces!' wailed Winnie. 'Whatever shall I do? You can't have a tea party without tea!'

Wilbur glanced at the clock.

'I know!' said Winnie. 'No time for shopping. I shall have to magic a new teapot. *Abracadabra!*'

And—**zing!**—there on the table was a beautiful big elephant teapot with a wavy trunk spout.

'Lovely!' said Winnie.

But when Winnie tried pouring tea from the trunk spout, it came out—**whoopsy-splosh**—jumping right over the cup to slosh on to the table.

'That's no blooming good!' said Winnie. 'Let's try again! *Abracadabra!*'

The next teapot's spout fell straight off, into the cup with the tea. The pot after that had its spout on a bit sideways so it poured tea to one side of the cup, all over the table and onto the floor. Winnie and Wilbur were wading in a sea of tea.

60

'Tea, tea everywhere, but not a drop to
drink!' said Winnie. 'Blooming stupid
magic!'

Grrrr-woof-ding-dong! nagged
the dooryell. **Woof-ding!**

'Flipping fishcakes, they're here, Wilbur!'

61

Winnie patted down her hair and
hurried to open the door. 'Oh, do come
in, Uncle Owen and Auntie Alice and
Cousin Cuthbert.'

Winnie pushed them all into her sitting
room. 'Sit yourselves down, all you
relative people. I've just got one teensy-
tadpole-toenail-sized little thing to see to
in the kitchen, if you'd like to chat among
yourselves for a moment or two.'

Winnie leapt back into the kitchen and started slamming plates down on the table. Wilbur was busy mopping up tea. They could overhear bits of conversation from the room next door.

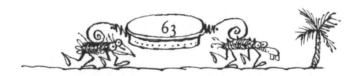

63

Uncle Owen said, 'Winnie will put me at the head of the table because I am the head of the family, being the oldest male here.'

'Ooer,' said Winnie. 'I'd better get that right.' She began to lay Uncle Owen's place at the head of the table.

'Oh, but I am older than you, Owen!' came Auntie Alice's voice. 'I always have been! Of course Winnie will put me at the head of the table!'

'Uh-oh!' muttered Winnie. 'Now, what do I do?'

Wilbur pointed to the other end.

'Good thinking, Wilbur!' said Winnie. 'A table has two ends!'

But now Cuthbert was complaining. 'I do have the highest magician degree among us, you know. I am the richest. So that makes me more important. Winnie will put . . .'

'. . . you all into highchairs for your tea, if you're not careful!' said Winnie. 'Whatever shall I . . . Ooo, I've got an idea, clever me! *Abracadabra!*'

67

And instantly she'd magicked a new table.

'We're ready!' said Winnie, 'Oh, except we still haven't got a teapot! Heck! Where's the glue, Wilbur?'

As quick as she could, Winnie stuck bits of teapot back into something like a teapot shape. But she could hear her guests talking again—

'Winnie will pour my cup of tea first,' said Owen. 'She knows that I'm the most important.'

'You're a knotty noodle, Owen!' said
Alice. 'Winnie will serve me first!'

'No, me of course!' said Cuthbert. 'Me,
me, me!'

'Silly things!' said Winnie. 'I'll soon
sort them! Where are those other pots,
Wilbur?'

At last Winnie was done, a bit gluey, a bit feathery, but ready for tea.

'Ahem,' she said as she went into the sitting room. 'Would you care to come through for tea now?'

Uncle Owen and Auntie Alice and Cousin Cuthbert all started pushing and pinching and . . .

'Behave yourselves!' said Winnie. 'You're all going to sit at the best place at the table . . . because the table is square!'

The relative people sat.

'Who would like tea?' asked Winnie.

'Me, me, me!' they all shouted (and not one of them said 'please').

'I shall pour you all the first cup of tea,' said Winnie. 'And I shall pour the first cup for myself as well.'

'Eh?' said the relative people as Winnie arranged four cups on the table. Then she took the cosy off her stuck-together pot, and she poured four cups of tea all at the same time.

'Oh!' said the relative people.

So everyone slurped and burped together and couldn't find much to quarrel about for the rest of teatime.

'Phew!' said Winnie as she closed the
door on her guests. 'Let's have another
cup, just the two of us this time, Wilbur.'

Winnie made a fresh pot of finest
ditchwater tea.

'Mrrow!' warned Wilbur, but Winnie
wasn't listening. She began to pour, and . . .

'A nice, hot tea footbath!' said Winnie,
dabbling her toes. 'The perfect way to
unwind after a busy day!'

Giddy-up,
WINNIE

'Come on, Dolly Drop!' shouted
Winnie, bouncing up and down on the
sofa and whacking it with her wand.
'Come on!'

She was watching horse racing on telly.

'Faster! Go on!'

Then a dreamy look came into Winnie's
eyes. 'Wouldn't it be wonderful to have a
horse and to go racing, Wilbur?'

'Mrrow!' Wilbur firmly shook his head.

Winnie's dreamy gaze wandered to her

wand, then to a rat on the floor. 'Wilbur, in *Cinderella* didn't they turn a rat into . . .? Ooo, yes!' Winnie waved her wand, *'Abracadabra!'*

'Neeeeiiggghhh!'

Suddenly there was a horse standing where the rat had been. It was big and cloppy and clumsy. **Crash!** Things began to fall as the horse turned around. **Scrunch! Tinkle! Smash!** Winnie's furniture and knick-knacks went flying.

'Steady, boy!' said Winnie. 'Er . . . you don't look very much like a racing horse. And that's not hay, you great cloppy twit! That's my hair! Earwigs' elbows, where can I put a horse where it won't do any harm? I think the kitchen's the best place.'

76

Winnie filled the sink with water for the horse. She fed it carrots and sugar lumps.

Chomp! Chomp! 'Blooming heck, that didn't last long! You'll have to win me some prize money if you want to keep eating expensive sugar lumps!'

78

Winnie put a blanket over the horse.
She tied him to a table leg. 'Go to sleep
now,' she said. 'You and I are going racing
in the morning!'

Winnie got into her nightie, and put her hair into a net. It did look a bit like black hay. Then she fell asleep, dreaming. 'Oh, thank you, your majesty,' she was telling the queen in her dream as she accepted a huge gold cup for winning the race. Then she was giving the horse a drink of champagne from the cup, and bubbles went up his nose and made him start to float, up and into the air, so Winnie caught hold of his tail and floated upwards too, and then ...

80

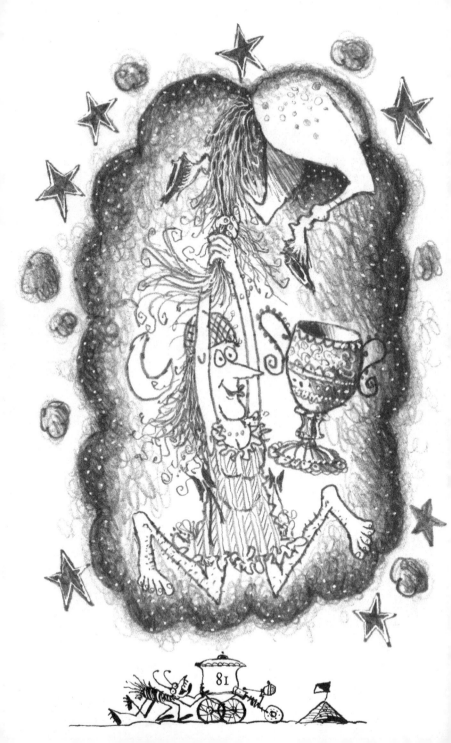

a horrible pong woke Winnie.

'Phewee! Hold your dose!' said Winnie,
clutching her nose as they went into the
kitchen.

'Neeeeiiggghhh!'

'Mrrow!'

There were piles of steaming horse poo
all over the floor.

Winnie grabbed her broom and started
to sweep it up, but the broom sulked and
kicked and flicked. 'This bit of having a
horse is no fun,' said Winnie. 'But racing
it will be as fun as an iced sherbet bun.
Let's get going!'

83

Winnie put on jockeyish clothes, with her smallest cauldron on her head as a hat.

'Hey, Wilbur, we need a proper racing kind of name for our horse. They are always called something stupid, aren't they? How about Whinnying Wonder?'

'Mrrow.' Wilbur wasn't impressed.

'Or Wilbur and Winnie's Winning Wonder? We can call him Four Ws for short.'

'Meeeow!'

So Winnie wrote '𝒲 𝒲 𝒲 𝒲 ' on a corner of the horse blanket.

'Now he looks as smart as a snoreberry tart!' said Winnie. 'Help me get up onto Four Ws, Wilbur, and then off we go!'

'Oooer! It's very high up!' said Winnie
when she was up. 'And he's as wide as a
whale to sit on. Ooo, me legs!'

Winnie clicked her tongue. 'Gee-up!'
Nothing happened.

Winnie dangled a sugar lump from the
end of her wand and waved it in front of
Four Ws. Four Ws stretched his neck,
snatched the sugar lump and scrunched
the end of the wand, but he didn't move.
Winnie kicked with her heels. Winnie
whacked with her broken wand. 'Get
moving, you great useless thing!' Still
nothing happened . . . until Winnie's
broomstick decided to help. The
broomstick gave Four Ws a great whack
on the bottom. **WHUMPH!**

'Neeeeiiggghhh!'

Up reared Four Ws, and then he was
off, galloping with great clip-cloppy
hooves out of Winnie's house, down the
road towards the race track.

'I didn't think he'd be this fast!' said
Winnie.

They didn't get very far. Wilbur clung
on to Four Ws' tail for as long as he could,
but he fell when Four Ws jumped the
garden gate. Winnie lasted a little longer,
but she soon somersaulted off to land—
CLANG!—on her cauldron helmet, then
bounced into a ditch full of smelly, green
goo slime.

'Oh, toads' bottom warts!' said Winnie,
pulling pondy creatures from her hair.

Winnie squelched sadly home to find
Wilbur busy stuffing mouse nests into the
foot of one of Winnie's pongy, holey old
socks.

'Whatever are you doing?' asked
Winnie, rubbing her bruises.

Wilbur pulled the sock over the top of Winnie's broomstick, and suddenly Winnie understood what he was doing. 'You're making a blooming hobby horse!' she said. 'Oo, you clever cat, you! More like a hobby zebra with those stripes!'

Winnie added half boiled-egg eyes and cabbage leaf ears to her broom hobby zebra horsey thing.

'Come on, Wilbur! If we're quick we can still make it for the last race!'

They hurried to the racetrack, hearing the cheers of the crowd and loudspeaker announcements as they got nearer—'The last race of the day is the all-comers' race. Horses to the paddock, please.'

'Quick!' said Winnie.

They joined the parade of horses and
jockeys around the ring. People pointed
and laughed at Winnie's horse.

'Take no notice!' said Winnie.

They lined up for the start. **Bang!**
And they were away! The proper horses
were galloping elegantly towards the first
jump with Winnie hobble-running
behind. Then she tripped and tumbled.

'Blasted bat bums!' said Winnie.

'Ha ha!' laughed the crowd.

'*Abracadabra!*' shouted Winnie.

Winnie's broomstick hobby zebra
horsey suddenly lifted Winnie and Wilbur
up, and charged fast after the galloping
horses. It swooped easily over the fence.
The broomstick hobby zebra horsey
turned and grinned his ghastly grin at the
horses coming up behind, and half of
them shied and swerved off-course.

'Giddy-up!' said Winnie, and on they
whizzed, before screeching to a halt over
the ditch, so all the other riders tried to
stop too and—**thump-bump!**—piled
into one another.

'Only one horse in front of us now!'
shouted Winnie. 'Come on, Broomy! I'll
never use you for sweeping horse poo
again if you win the race!'

The broomstick doubled its speed and
became a blur, winning the race by just
one smelly stuffed sock head's length.

'Hooray!' shouted Winnie.

'Hooray!' shouted the crowd.

'You can't have the winning cup,' said the snooty man in the hat. 'That's only for riders of real horses.'

'I don't mind,' said Winnie. 'I've got my own prize.' And she took something from her pocket, popped it into her mouth and began to scrunch. 'That's the best thing about a hobby horse.' She patted Broomy on the nose. 'You can eat the sugar lumps yourself!'

Enjoy more magic moments with
Winnie AND **Wilbur**